Wild Robert

Diana Wynne Jones

Wild Robert

Illustrated by
Emma Chichester Clark

Collins
An imprint of HarperCollinsPublishers

First published by Methuen Children's Books 1989
First published in paperback by Collins 2001
Collins is an imprint of HarperCollins*Publishers* Ltd
77-85 Fulham Palace Road, Hammersmith,
London, W6 8JB

The HarperCollins website address is:
www.**fireandwater**.com

3 5 7 9 8 6 4 2

Text copyright © Diana Wynne Jones 1989
Illustrations copyright © Emma Chichester Clark 1989

ISBN 0 00 675524 0

The author and illustrator assert the moral right to be
identified as the author and illustrator of the work.

Printed and bound in Great Britain by
Omnia Books Limited, Glasgow

Chapter One

Heather was in a bad mood. Her bicycle was broken, right at the start of the summer holidays, too, and this meant that she could not ride down to see her friend Janine in the village. It was five miles to the village. Either Heather could walk, five miles there and five miles back, or she could stay at home. And home was not really home – or not in the summer anyway. Heather lived in a stately home called Castlemaine, because her mum and dad were curators there.

In summer, every day at eleven-thirty, the car park at the side of the old stables began to fill with cars, vans and coaches, and tourists climbed out of them and spread all over the house and gardens. There was almost nowhere that was private. And Heather's mum and dad were far too busy showing people round the house, or coping with sudden emergencies, to be any company for Heather.

That day, Heather made a mistake about the time. She looked up from the book she had been gloomily reading since breakfast and thought the clock said ten-thirty. Good, she thought. That would give her an hour to get to a really private hiding place before the tourists came. She thought she would go to the very top of the old castle tower, because that was supposed to be unsafe for crowds. There she could read her book, or look out over the hills and woody valleys while she ate her lunch. It was not as good as being with Janine, but it was not a bad place on a fine day. You could not see the tourists from there, and hardly even hear them.

But first she had to get some lunch. Heather went to the small kitchen, behind the huge whitewashed kitchen the tourists were shown, and opened the fridge there.

"Bother!" she said. If she wanted sandwiches, there was a choice between tuna fish and spam, and they were out of tomatoes again. To get tomatoes, or fruit, she would have to go to the gardens and be polite to surly old Mr McManus the gardener. Heather decided she could not face his bad temper. She would go to Mrs Mimms, who kept the tourist shop, and ask her for crisps or biscuits instead. She hated Mr McManus even more than she hated spam.

She made herself six tuna sandwiches and put them in a bag. She was just fetching her book from the big tourist kitchen when voices rang out somewhere near. She heard the grind and crunch of wheels through the thick white walls.

"Oh, no!" Heather said. She ran out into the passage that overlooked the parking space. Through the diamond-pane windows there she could see quite a number of cars parked already and at least one coach. Another coach lumbered in as she looked, and people carrying cameras jumped down from it. "Why have they all come so *early*?" Heather said, still not realising she had made a mistake with the time.

She knew she couldn't get to Mrs Mimms' shop before those people from the coach crowded into it to buy ice-creams. She set off for the tower at once instead, by the easy back way that brought her out on a high gallery, looking down on the round room beside the stone steps up to the tower. But she was too late. Even before she got to the gallery, Heather heard the shuffle of tourists' feet. Her father's voice rang out.

"We are now in part of the old castle. It was built by the first baron, Hugh Toller, early in the twelfth century. These stone stairs behind me lead to the watch-tower built by Hugh Toller's son William."

Heather leant over the rail of the balcony and looked down on packed heads with the faces all turned towards Dad. Dad was talking away, posed with one foot on the tower steps. Heather was in time to see him reach out expertly and grab the boy who had tried to sneak behind the red rope across the steps.

"No, sonny, you can't go up. The tower's unsafe and we can't get insurance. By 1150, the castle was already quite large..."

Heather turned away. "Sheep," she muttered. "Beastly sheep in the way." She knew Dad was quite capable of going on talking until Mum or one of the other guides came along with the next party. She was cut off from the tower. And by now the coach party would be filling the entrance hall and waiting to be taken up the main stairs.

Heather ducked down a side passage and ran. If she went through the Long Gallery and the Feud Room, she might be able to make it to the back stairs before any tourists did. She raced along the polished floor of the Long Gallery, where white reproachful faces of dead Tollers stared out of thick gilt frames at her. She was just going to turn into the Feud Room, when feet shuffled again. This time Heather heard her mother's voice.

"We are now coming into the small gallery known as the Feud Room. This is because the portraits of the Tollers on your left and the portraits of the Franceys on your right are those of the two branches of the family who kept up a long and hostile quarrel for nearly one hundred years…"

"More beastly sheep!" Heather said. She turned and looked at the big clock above the picture of Sir Francis Toller bowing to Queen Elizabeth I. It said five to twelve. She understood her mistake now.

"Oh *bother*!" she said. "I hate tourists! I hate living at Castlemaine!"

She went back through the Long Gallery and down the main stairs. Halfway down, she met the

next party of tourists coming up. It was like wading
in a stream with the current the wrong way. Heather
turned sideways and wriggled and fought her way
down into the entrance hall. A glance was enough to
show her that the shop at the side was crowded out
and that Mrs Mimms was too busy to spare Heather
a look, let alone any biscuits. Heather wandered
gloomily out through the main door. Mr Mimms,
sitting at his desk there to take tickets, did spare her
a smile and a nod, but Heather was feeling so
dismal by then that it did not help much.

She wandered on, into the formal gardens. Here
there were some girls and boys her own age eating
ice lollies and dropping the wrappers on the gravel
path. "They wouldn't dare do that at home!"

12

Heather muttered, and she took care to pass them in the distance. She went on into the walled garden, where Mr McManus usually was. Since things were so horrible anyway, she thought she might as well ask him for a tomato.

The walled garden, for some reason, was always the place where the elderly couples went. Heather passed one set, where the lady was saying, "See, Harry. This one is the old thornless rose." Then there was another foursome, where a man was lecturing the other three about pruning roses. And a third pair, where the lady was hooting, "That is simply not the way to plant roses! If the gardener here was mine, I'd soon tell him where to get off!"

She was sure Mr McManus could hear this lady from the corner where he was working. When Heather found him, he was raking a seedbed as if it were the throat of an old lady.

"Get you gone!" he said to Heather.

"I only wanted to ask—" Heather began.

"Laying down the law, tramping my lawns, messing up my paths with packets and papers and gum," said Mr McManus. "Screaming, asking things—"

"I hate tourists too," said Heather. "There's no need to take it out on me."

"Leaving bottles and tins," said Mr McManus. "You're worse than all the rest. Get you gone!"

This was so unfair that all Heather could think of to do was to stump away through the nearest door, with her mouth pressed tight, hoping Mr McManus would tread on a rake and get concussion. She turned the corner into the ruined temple. Usually, nobody found the way there. But today was a bad day. Some very large and grown-up teenagers had found the temple and they were romping there among the pillars and the green mounds. Heather slithered on past, skirting a fallen statue where a pair of the teenagers were kissing, and plunged into the woods behind the temple.

She only knew one other place that was likely to be private. This was the peculiar little mound right on the edge of the Castlemaine grounds. When

Heather and her parents had first moved to Castlemaine, Mum had been very excited about this mound. She said it was surely an ancient Bronze Age burial mound. Then Heather had gone to school in the village and met Janine. Janine told Heather that it was the grave of a man from the olden days who had been accused of doing witchcraft. He was called Wild Robert and everyone in the village knew about him. They said there was a box of treasure buried with him. This made Heather as excited as Mum. She went to Dad and suggested they hunted for the treasure.

Dad smiled kindly, in the way he had, and looked at the old maps of Castlemaine. "Sorry to disappoint you both," he said to Heather and Mum. "You know what that mound really is? It's an ice-house. They used to keep ice in a sort of cave inside the mound, so that the Tollers and Franceys could have ice-cream in summer. I dare say if we dug in it, we'd find the cave still there."

After that, the mound seemed rather dull. Mum forgot about it and Heather only went there at times like today, when there seemed to be tourists everywhere else.

Or *was* it dull? she wondered as she walked towards it. It was hidden in a mass of yew trees. Heather's feet made almost no sound as she ploughed through the soft piles of yellow needles.

And there was something about the light that filtered through the dark black-green of the needles overhead. It made everything look sort of smoky. The mound itself reared up into this smokiness, bald and covered with yew needles. Not dull, Heather thought. More as if this is not a nice place to be.

She climbed the mound and sat down. She opened her book. But it was too dark under the yew trees to read.

Somehow, this was the last straw. Heather banged the soft earth with her fist. "Oh, bother it all!" she cried out. "Wild Robert, I just wish you were really under there. You could come out and deal with the tourists and teach Mr McManus some manners!"

The sun came out overhead. That seemed to make the mist under the trees smokier than ever. The smell of it was strange, like earth and spices. It rolled over Heather in waves. Out of it, a voice said, "Did somebody call?"

Chapter Two

"**D**id somebody call?" the voice said again. It was a husky voice. Heather thought it must be one of the teenage boys from the temple. She did not answer. But the voice said, "Didn't somebody call?"

"Well – sort of," Heather said. "I was just talking really."

There was a noise somewhere below that sounded like someone crawling through undergrowth. Heather stood up nervously. She was fairly sure the person had mistaken her for one of his friends. Unless she ran away quickly, it was going to be very awkward. But she could not see where he was and she did not want to run straight into him. She stood where she was, looking anxiously round into the smoky mist. And the person took her by surprise by standing up in front of her to dust yew-needles off his tight black clothes.

"There. So, here I am," he said cheerfully.

He was not one of the ones by the temple. He was the oldest kind of teenager, or perhaps even a young man. Heather was never quite sure when people changed over from one to the other. He was very good-looking. He had fairish, wavy hair that came to his shoulders and huge dark eyes set a little slanting in his smooth dark face – in fact, he was so good-looking that it made up for his not being very tall. He was only a head higher than Heather. She thought, from his clothes, that he must have come here on a motorcycle, although he had a big white collar spread over the shoulders of his black jacket, which puzzled her a little.

"Did you come to see round the house, or are you just exploring?" she asked him politely.

The young man laughed. "No, sweetheart, I came because you called. It is always so. The words Bishop Henry laid on me were never so heavy that I could not hear my name when it was said."

"I – I beg your pardon?" said Heather.

"What date is it?" the young man asked.

"Er – nineteen eighty-nine," said Heather. She was beginning to feel alarmed. Either the young man was mad, or something very odd had happened.

The young man seemed even more alarmed. He stared at her, and she could see he had gone pale by the black way his eyes stood out in his face. "No!" he said. "Oh, no! Then that makes three hundred and fifty years shut in the mound!" He put his hand on Heather's arm appealingly. "Tell me not that so much time has passed."

His hand felt – strange. It was chilly, but it was warm too, and it somehow fizzed against Heather's bare arm so that all the hairs stood up round the place he touched. Heather backed away. The feel of his hand, even more than what he said, made her fairly sure he was not mad, and even surer that something very odd indeed had happened. "Who are you?" she said.

The young man laughed again, in the bright way people laugh when their feelings are hurt. "My name is Robert Toller," he said.

"*Wild* Robert?" Heather said from behind both hands, which had somehow leapt to cover her mouth. "The one who – who was supposed to do witchcraft?"

Robert Toller looked definitely hurt now. "And so I can," he said. "Why else should my half-brother call a bishop to put me down? They knew I had studied the magic arts and were persuaded I meant to take their heritage from them – though I meant them nothing but kindness." He looked more hurt than ever for a moment. Then a thought struck him. His slanting eyes turned to Heather, sideways and warily. "Are the present-day Tollers likely to think the same? Who holds Castlemaine now?"

"Well – no one really," Heather said. "The last of the Tollers died out a long time ago. And then it went to the Franceys, and the last Francey died six years ago and left everything to the British Trust. My mum and dad look after it for the Trust."

Heather was not sure how much of this Robert Toller took in. While she was speaking, he almost looked as if he might cry. But that look was pushed aside by a bright smile and a fierce sort of delight. Before she had finished explaining, he was laughing wildly and hugging himself with both arms.

"Oh, splendid news!" he cried out. "Then I am the only Toller living! Castlemaine is mine after all!" He stopped laughing and explained to Heather, rather anxiously, "I *am* in line to inherit. My father was the younger Francis and he married my mother when his first wife died."

Heather nodded. She could see how sad he was

really and she did not want to hurt his feelings any more, but she could not help wondering how Robert Toller was going to explain to the people who ran the British Trust. And I bet he doesn't have a birth certificate! she thought. I don't think they were invented in his day.

While she wondered what she *could* say, Robert Toller gave her a little bow and stuck out one elbow to her. "Come," he said. "Let us leave this dismal wood and take a look at my heritage."

Heather knew he meant her to take hold of his elbow in an elegant way, but the strange fizzing she had felt when he touched her made her scared to try. Robert Toller smiled. He had a very winning smile, as good-looking as the rest of him.

"Walk with me," he said, "and tell me your name." And he waited, holding his elbow out and keeping the smile until it looked quite strained.

Heather found she simply could not bear to hurt his feelings any more. "My name's Heather Bayley," she said. She picked up her book and her bag of lunch and put her hand on his elbow – his sleeve was black silk, not the leather she had taken it for – and it fizzed. But she got used to it quite quickly and let him help her slither down the mound.

They walked under the yew trees and Heather felt quite grand and old-fashioned. She noticed that Robert Toller, in spite of his black clothes, seemed to

stand out strong and bright in the smoky light. She looked down at herself and found that her own legs, and her hand on Robert Toller's elbow, looked much greyer and dimmer. When they came out into the sunlight, Robert Toller looked brighter still. It was as if he was somehow twice as alive as ordinary people. Heather was staring at him, thinking about this, when they came to the ruined temple.

The teenagers were still there, romping about. Heather wondered how she could ever have thought Robert Toller was one of them. He stood out as quite different, now she saw them. Three of the

24

girls were up on the fallen statue throwing empty
coke cans at the boys. Robert Toller stopped dead
and stared at them. Heather looked at the black
leather mini-skirts and the tall punk hairstyles and
suddenly saw that they must seem outrageous to
someone from three hundred and fifty years ago.

But it was not that. Robert Toller had gone white
again. He said, "This I will not have! This temple
was where my father met with my mother." And he
shouted at the teenagers, "Get you gone! Go riot in
some other place!" They all looked round at him, a
bit surprised. Then they laughed and went back to

pelting one another with cans. Robert Toller's face bunched up. His lower lip stuck out. He looked exactly like a very small boy who was just about to burst into tears, but Heather was fairly sure he was very angry. He spread one hand out palm down in front of him, and muttered something under his breath. Then he tipped his hand slowly sideways. "Go riot, then, until I bid all stop," he said.

Heather felt as if something tipped with Robert's hand. It was as if the part of the world that was ordinary and possible went slanting away sideways in a thin sheet. One edge of the thin sheet went upwards, and the other sloped down through the harder, stranger part of the world that was always underneath, leaving that part bare. Heather actually saw the grey edge tip and travel across the sunny grass and the white stone pillars and the laughing girls and boys. For a moment, she was sure she was standing out sideways, somehow, on the slice of ordinariness. Then she found she was on the deeper bit after all.

And, as the grey edge passed across the teenagers, each of them changed. The boys lost their shirts and jackets and grew brown fur instead of trousers. The girls grew tousled long hair and even more tousled long dresses, with ivy leaves wound round them. The cans they were holding became metal goblets. All of them shouted at once:

"IO!"

After that the girls screamed and ran and the boys ran after them on twinkling little hooves. Before Heather had come out of standing sideways, they were chasing madly through the wood, crying out to one another in a strange language.

As their screams and shouts faded into the distance, Robert Toller turned to Heather with a pleased smile, like a small boy who has got his own way. "There. Now you know I can indeed use the magic art," he said. "Those will romp until sundown releases them."

"Yes, but—" said Heather. She wanted to say all sorts of things, but all she could manage was, "Why did you do *that*?"

Robert seemed surprised. "I told you," he said. "This temple was where my father used to meet in secret with my mother, in the days before they were married. See, I will show you." He strode across the beautifully mown grass, past the fallen statue, to where the slender white pillars gathered into a shape that was almost like a house. There was a block of stone there, embedded in the turf, which looked as if it had once been part of a roof above the pillars. Maybe it had once had carvings on it. At any rate, Heather could see some sort of pattern on the side of it, worn with age and covered with green mildew.

"See," Robert said, and smoothed his hand across the old worn shapes.

It was as if his hand brought the stone into focus. It became clear and white and new. The carving was a sort of figure-eight shape that looked as if it was intended to be a piece of rope with a capital letter carved on either side of it. The letter on the left was a large plain F. The one on the right was a curlier E.

"They carved their initials here," Robert said, "together with a true-love knot. Francis was my father's name. My mother was called Eglantine."

He was looking beyond the stone into the square of green turf enclosed by the white pillars. Heather looked there too and, just for an instant, it seemed to her that there were two people there, walking gladly towards one another as if they had not seen each other for a very long time. The man was taller and burlier than Robert, though his hair was the same colour. The woman was small – tiny – and she seemed all floating: floating hair, floating clothes. Heather only saw them for the length of time it took them each to stretch an arm out to the other. Then she was not sure she had seen them at all. She looked at Robert to ask him, but he had turned away, smiling fiercely, and the stone was blurred and green again.

"Let us sit on this stone," he said. "There are savoury smells from that bag you carry that remind me I have not eaten for more than three centuries."

"It's only tuna fish," said Heather.

Chapter Three

Robert Toller seemed so hungry that Heather took one sandwich herself and let him have all the rest. He kept saying it was the best food he had ever eaten – which made Heather feel a bit silly, because it *was* only tuna fish, after all. While he was wolfing the sandwiches down, Heather kept hearing distant shouts and yells from the teenagers in the wood. She told herself that they had deserved what happened to them, but this did not stop her feeling quite uncomfortable about it. She decided she liked Robert, and she knew she was sorry for him, waking up to find so much time had passed, but she was still uncomfortable.

To take her mind off it, she said, "People in the village say there was some treasure buried with you."

That was an unwise thing to say. Robert gave her a sideways look. "They still say that, do they?" Heather could tell he had gone very cautious. She tried to say that it was just something she had *heard*, and not important, but he interrupted her with a

laugh. It was the hurt laugh again, Heather saw. "And who am I to say what men will call a treasure?" he said. Then he jumped up briskly and said, "Eating fish is dry work. I could do with some fruit."

"There are strawberries and redcurrants ripe in the kitchen garden," Heather said, "but they're supposed to be for sale. I don't think Mr McManus will let us have any."

"McManus?" Robert said. "That was a name you said when you called me up. What right has he to sell fruit from Castlemaine?"

"He's the gardener," Heather explained. "The

money from the fruit helps pay for the house."

"I see," said Robert. He said it very grimly, as if Heather had explained something quite different. Before she could say any more, he was striding to the door in the walled garden.

She caught up when Robert stopped, right in the middle, staring round at the rose arches, and the rose bushes, and the roses trained up the walls. "What is this?" he said. "Not a herb in sight! It is all roses!"

Heather understood how strange things must be to him. She said kindly, "Dad told me they made this into a rose garden about a hundred years ago. The kitchen garden's through that door in the wall over there."

"Then it has changed about," Robert said. "The roses used to be through there." He strode towards the door. On the way to it he passed several pairs of the usual elderly people. Heather was afraid he was going to ask them what they were doing there, but he walked straight past them, giving each pair a cool nod, as if in his day you expected to see people about. The elderly people stared a bit, but they nodded back politely. All the same, Heather was relieved when they reached the kitchen garden and went through the door marked NO ADMITTANCE TO THE PUBLIC.

"Ah!" said Robert Toller.

The strawberry beds stretched right across the
garden, with lines of currant bushes on either side.
They were neatly spread with straw. Giant red
berries gleamed on the straw, under the leaves and
crowns of white flowers. Robert crunched out into
the straw and began picking strawberries as fast as
he could go. "I do not remember strawberries so
big!" he remarked to Heather over his shoulder.
And when Heather had, rather timidly, crunched
out to join him, he added with his mouth full, "Time
was when I thought I would never taste one again."

Mr McManus had an instinct about people
picking fruit. Heather had just picked her first

strawberry when Mr McManus crashed out from the left-hand line of currant bushes with a roar. "Get out of that! You leave those berries alone, you, or I'll have you arrested for stealing!"

Robert calmly picked another strawberry and stood up with it, raising his eyebrows. "Stealing?" he said. "I have a right to pick my own berries, surely? And if we are to talk of stealing, I have known other gardeners before you who took Castlemaine fruit and sold it as their own."

Heather tried to crawl away backwards into the currant bushes. This was awful! Robert had misunderstood. But she stopped when she saw that

Mr McManus's mottled brown face had turned a sort of mottled soap-colour. That was interesting. It looked as if Mr McManus really had been taking fruit. But of course this made Mr McManus angrier than ever. He plodded towards Robert with his teeth showing.

"You'll prove nothing!" he said, grunting with fury. "Get out of here or I'll tear your smooth face off! I don't care who you are!"

Robert popped the strawberry into his mouth and spread his hand out in front of him again. This time he tipped only ever so slightly. Mr McManus still tried to plod towards him, but now he was plodding on the spot, rather like a tortoise that doesn't know it has come to the end of the string tied to its shell.

"But you *should* care who I am," Robert said, when he had swallowed the strawberry. "My brother had that other gardener whipped from our gates. Castlemaine is mine now, and I should do worse to you, for your snarls and threats. But for now I shall leave you as you are. Come, Heather. Help yourself to my fine fruit."

Robert bent down and started picking strawberries again. After a little while, Heather came out of the bushes and picked strawberries too. This was the only time she had ever been able to do this. But she wished she was enjoying it more. The plod-plod-plodding figure of Mr McManus made her feel like a thief, or worse. Every time one of them crawled near him, he shouted, "I'll get you for this! You won't get away with it!" Heather grabbed strawberries with both hands every time he shouted. She knew she would never be given another chance to eat as many as she wanted.

At last, when Mr McManus's tramping boots had worn quite a hole in the earth, Robert Toller stood up and dusted straw from his black silk knees. "I have had my fill," he said. "Come and show me my house and castle now."

Heather thought of Castlemaine full of tourists and the coaches parked at the side. She knew it would be a terrible shock to him. "Why don't you wait until this evening?" she said. "It'll be much more peaceful."

Robert gave her a strange sad look, almost as if he was sorry for her. "Sweetheart, I know those tricks," he said. "And by then, all will be straight and tidy because you are bound to warn your father I am here. No, my time to see the place is now."

He crunched across the straw, past Mr McManus. "You won't get away with this!" Mr McManus snarled. "I'll have the law—"

"Oh, be quiet, you cur, you growling dog!" Robert said. He spread his hand out again, and this time he tipped it sharply. Heather saw the line of the world slant past her eyes like the top of the water when someone ducks you in the swimming pool. She felt rather as if she had been ducked, too. While she was gasping for air, Mr McManus fell on his hands and knees and shrank. His mottled face grew into the long muzzle of a large spotted dog. His legs bunched up and became the hind legs of a dog. His hands grew into paws and he sprouted a long spotted tail. He growled nastily at Robert.

"Leave this place, you mongrel!" Robert said. "Go home and see if your wife knows you."

The ugly spotted dog tucked its tail between its mottled back legs and raced away into the bushes, howling. Heather had never seen a dog look so frightened. She led the way to the house, not quite as amused or as pleased as she expected to be. True, Mr McManus deserved it, but Heather kept finding herself wondering if Mrs McManus *would* know who the dog was.

Chapter Four

The formal gardens were crowded with people by this time. For a while, Robert Toller hardly seemed to notice. He was staring at the house. Heather thought his stare had a lost sort of look to it, but when Robert noticed her watching him, he made his face look proud and amused.

"By horn and hoof!" he said. "What a splendid pile of a building this has become! It seems I inherit a house with a hundred windows or more! How did this come about?"

"The Franceys and the Tollers kept adding bits to make it grander," Heather explained. "I think Dad said they only stopped when one of them betted all the money that Napoleon would win Waterloo." She saw that Robert did not understand this, so she added comfortingly, "But the older bits are still there, really."

Robert nodded. "I see the shape of my father's house sketched along one side," he said. "And our old stables are there still, beyond the kitchens. But I only see one tower out of all the castle where I used

to scramble with my brothers."

"There's more of it than that," Heather said, "but it's sort of built into the inside now."

"I must see," Robert said.

Heather could tell he had enjoyed climbing about the castle with his brothers. She envied him rather. She had often thought that she would have enjoyed living in Castlemaine more with a brother or sister or so to keep her company. But then it came to her that Robert's brothers must have been dead now for three hundred years. And the house was quite changed since his day. She found she did not envy Robert any longer.

While she was thinking this, Robert had begun to walk faster and faster towards the house. Heather spotted his strangely bright figure some way ahead. As the crowds were thickest nearer the house, she could see him bumping into people and bouncing off others. She could hear cries of, "Steady on!" and, "Who do you think you're shoving?" That seemed to make Robert notice what he was doing. He stopped and waited for Heather. When she caught up at last, she found he was looking very haughty.

"Your father keeps a mighty big court here," he said. "Who gave him permission to have so many followers?"

"They're not followers. They're tourists," Heather said. She took Robert on a walk through the box hedges while she did her best to explain how Castlemaine now belonged to the British Trust, which meant that anyone in the country could pay to see round the grounds.

Robert walked beside her, nodding and frowning and narrowing his eyes. Heather could see he was doing his best to look businesslike, but she had a strong feeling that he had never done anything businesslike in his life. "I do not see how a house can stand without an owner," he said.

As luck would have it, a crowd of schoolchildren stampeded in among the box hedges just then, shouting and eating ice lollies. Heather could tell they were a party from a school that had not broken up yet. They all wore blue uniform blazers and they were followed by a teacher who was shouting even louder than they were.

"You are to walk, not run, Two X!" the teacher screamed.

She was the kind of teacher nobody listens to. The children went on shouting and ran round and round the pond in the middle, forcing Heather and Robert to back away into the tall hedge at the end.

"Silence!" shrieked the teacher. And when that made no difference at all, she howled, "You are all to come and put your ice-cream wrappers in this litter bin this instant!"

The only difference this made was that each child promptly threw away his or her wrapper wherever he or she happened to be. Wrappers snowed across the paths, draped themselves over hedges and strewed on the flower-beds behind the hedges. The pond in the middle was thick with floating papers, showing lime-green or raspberry-red or chocolate-brown faces labelled Mr Lolly.

"Pick up these papers at once!" the teacher yelled.

No one seemed to hear her.

Robert stared. "Is this a school for the deaf?" he asked Heather.

"No, it's just a feeble teacher," Heather said.

"You mean, she does not take the whip to them often enough?" Robert said. Before Heather could explain that teachers did not generally whip people these days, Robert said, "Then I must teach her a lesson along with her pupils." He stretched out his hand. He tipped it. Heather seemed to feel the edge of the world rustle as it peeled past her ears – a soggy sort of rustle, like wet paper. She swallowed, because it made her ears pop.

In the pond, a lime-green ice lolly wrapper began to grow. It spread swiftly, somehow eating up all the other wrappers it came to, bigger and bigger, like a giant water lily leaf. Before anyone could blink, it was too big for the pond and lay across it, curling and uncurling its edges. The monstrous lime-green face on it glared. It opened a giant chocolate-coloured mouth to show raspberry-red teeth. A huge voice from it roared, "SILENCE! PICK UP THOSE WRAPPINGS!"

The teacher screamed and ran away. The children all stood where they were, staring uncertainly. "It's just a TV stunt," one of them said. "Take no notice."

Robert grinned. His little finger and his thumb tipped, ever so slightly.

"IS THAT SO?" roared the lime-green Mr Lolly. And it rose out of the pond, huger than ever, dripping water, and grabbed for the nearest children with torn, wet, green paper hands. Most of them backed away.

Most of them looked quite frightened, but there were one or two who began laughing scornfully.

"Kick it in the teeth," a boy said. "It's only paper."

Robert's face bunched up and his lower lip came out. His thumb twitched sharply, twice. All the rest of the paper strewn over the paths and the hedges and the flower-beds flew into the air and gathered into two large rustling clots. Next second, a raspberry-coloured Mr Lolly and a chocolate-coloured one were stalking across the hedges towards the boy. The expressions on their vast faces were of pure hatred. Heather was not surprised when the boy turned and ran. And once he was running, all the other children panicked as well and ran after him, crashing through the little hedges, trampling on the flower-beds and pushing one another to get away from the three gigantic figures stalking after them.

Robert lowered his hand and watched the pink and the green and the brown figures march out of sight beyond the bushes. "There," he said. "They will chase them to the edge of my estate. And woe betide the child they catch."

Heather had often wished something like this would happen to all the children who dropped wrappers at Castlemaine. Yet she could not help saying, "Don't let any of them get caught – please!"

Robert laughed. "What a tender heart you have!" he said. "Very well. They shall be pursued but never

quite caught, to show them that I will not suffer rubbish to be thrown upon my gardens. Castlemaine is not a fairground or a market-place. It is my home."

Heather saw he still did not understand. She explained again, as well as she could, how the last of the Franceys had left Castlemaine, in a very ruined state, to the British Trust in his will. And how the Trust had repaired it all and put it on show, with Heather's dad to look after it.

Robert turned and led the way into the rest of the gardens. "Yes, I follow that your father is by way of being seneschal or steward to my family," he said, "but I think he must find another way to fill his purse. It is not seemly to have all this prying into our grounds and our rooms."

"It's not Dad's purse, it's for the *upkeep!*" Heather said, quite exasperated by now. She had the feeling she was explaining things to a very small child, who was being deliberately stupid. "Don't you understand that Castlemaine needs *thousands* of pounds every year for repairs, and stopping the roof leaking and so on? I've heard Mum and Dad doing the accounts. They get the money from the people who come to see the house. They *need* them."

Robert snapped his fingers crossly. "No longer," he said. "Take me to your father and I will tell him to find money another way."

"What? You mean from your treasure?" Heather asked.

Robert gave her another sideways look. "You harp on that," he said. "No, I must speak with your father. Meanwhile all these folk must go away home."

"But—" Heather began, and stopped with a gulp, because she saw the line of the world waving up and down in front of her eyes. The path under her feet seemed to slant first one way and then another, even though she knew it was not moving, and she saw the flowers and hedges rippling. It made her wish she had not eaten quite so many strawberries.

When things straightened out, Heather saw that all the people round her were quietly heading towards the car park. A mother and father went by with four small children. The father was saying, "I think we've seen all there is to see here."

"We've been here too long," the mother agreed. "The kids aren't the only ones who are bored stiff."

Though this was exactly what Heather had been wishing for, only this morning, she found she was horrified. Robert had spoilt a day out for hundreds of people. And if he went on sending people away, day after day, Castlemaine would have no money at all. Maybe Mum and Dad would lose their jobs. She looked round for Robert to explain to him, but he was nowhere near. His oddly bright figure was a long way ahead, striding through the steady stream of people all making for the car park. He was nearly at the house.

Heather raced after him, dodging past people and bumping into others. By the time she reached the steps to the main door, Robert was most of the way up them. "Wait!" she panted.

But he did not wait. He went straight indoors and straight past the desk where Mr Mimms sat taking tickets. Mr Mimms said, "May I see your ticket for the tour of the house, sir?" And when Robert went straight past without taking any notice, Mr Mimms sighed and began levering himself up.

"He's with me, Mr Mimms," Heather panted as she shot past. Mr Mimms had only one leg. Heather liked Mr Mimms. She did not want him turned into another dog. Besides, she had once seen a dog with three legs and felt desperately sorry for it. She was glad when Mr Mimms believed her and sat down again.

Ahead of her there was a big party of people gathering in the hall for the next tour of the house. Robert had not sent them home, but he had somehow dodged through them. Heather could see his clear, bright shape climbing the main stairs. "Excuse me," Heather said, pushing among the waiting people. "Excuse me." And when some of the people took no notice, she put on a whining voice and lied shamelessly. "I've *got* to find my Mum! She's up those stairs."

They let her through and she dashed up the stairs, thinking it would just serve her right if she did run into Mum. Mum was probably the last person she wanted to meet – apart from Dad, that was – at least until she had thought of some way to stop Robert working magic all over the place. And even then there was the problem of what he was going to do for the rest of his life, she realised. She clattered up the stairs trying to think of jobs for magicians. All she could think of was a magic show on television. And wouldn't Robert hate that?

She caught up with Robert outside the bedroom Queen Elizabeth I slept in. He was peering inside wonderingly. "What is the reason for the red rope across the doorway?" he asked her. "Is there danger beyond?"

"No, it's because Queen Elizabeth I slept there," Heather said. "The room's full of treasures. Now *look*—!"

"But she never used *this* room!" Robert said. "They told me how a place was made for her downstairs. She was old then, and stairs troubled her." And when Heather opened her mouth again to scold him, he gave her another of his odd sideways looks and said, "What strange things are called treasures! I see no treasure here but the coverlet my grandmother stitched for my brother's wedding."

"Well that's a treasure because she stitched it so beautifully!" Heather snapped. "Now *listen* to me! You had no business sending those people home. They'd all paid to *be* here!"

Robert shrugged. "This is a matter I shall discuss with your father," he said. "Where is he?"

Heather knew she needed a lot more time to think before she let Robert anywhere near Dad.

She thought of herself saying to Dad, "This is Wild Robert. I just happened to call him up out of his mound." And she knew just the kind, unbelieving look Dad would give her, and how he would try to hide a smile. Then she thought of Robert getting angry and turning Dad into a dog. She even knew the lean, brown, trusting sort of dog that Dad would turn into. No – she would have to do a lot of thinking before she let them get together.

"Last time I saw my father," she said truthfully, "he was by the stairs to William Toller's tower."

Robert's face brightened. "The old watch-tower! How do we go there these days?"

"Through the Long Gallery," said Heather, and took him that way.

Robert was delighted with the Long Gallery. "This is almost as I remember!" he said, looking through one of the line of leaded windows. "And the view of the garden is not so strange, either! I can almost begin to think myself at home. Except—" He waved towards the rows of pictures in their fat gilt frames. "Except for these strangers. Who are they all?"

Heather seized on the chance to side-track him. She took Robert along the pictures and told him about all the ones she could remember the names of. "This is Lady Mary Francey," she said. "I know her because she's so pretty. And the bishop is Henry Toller. And here's James Toller in the curly wig. This

one with the gun is Edward Toller-Francey – I think he was killed in a war."

As she went, she kept noticing a very mixed expression on Robert's face. Heather thought she understood. Some of it was pride, some of it was the lost look she had noticed when Robert first saw the house. She thought she would feel very odd, too, looking at all the people who came after her in her own family. None of them looked much like Robert. Some of them had dark eyes and light hair, but none of them had the brown, slanted features of Robert's face.

"There isn't a picture of you, is there?" she said, as they came round under the picture of Sir Francis bowing to Queen Elizabeth I.

The mixed feelings on Robert's face gave way to a bright smile Heather somehow did not believe in. She knew he was hurt again. "There would be none," he said. "I had my portrait done, but I daresay it was burnt when I – when I was put down. My brother married a lady strongly puritan, who detested my magic arts." His bright smile stretched even brighter. "She was a Francey, as it happens." As if he was glad to change the subject, he swung round and pointed to the smaller gallery. "And here is another room of pictures that is new to me."

"That's the Feud Room," Heather said. She was glad to change the subject, too. "It's the pictures of all the Franceys and Tollers who had the quarrel two hundred years ago."

Robert hugged himself with both arms and burst out laughing. He laughed with his head thrown back until the Long Gallery rang with it. "Oh, this is great! I put a curse on them, that Franceys should hate Tollers, in revenge on my brother's wife. And it took! It took! What did they quarrel about?"

"Hush," said Heather. "I've no idea. I just know there were duels and lawsuits and things for a hundred years."

Robert turned to her with that look a person has when they are going to be thoroughly naughty. "Shall we find out?" He spread his hand out.

Heather surprised herself by saying *"No!"* as sternly as Mum did sometimes.

But it was too late.

Chapter Five

The edge of the ordinary world tipped past
Heather's eyes and strangeness took over. All
down the Feud Room the glass of pictures swung
open like windows. The first person to lean out of his
frame was a man in a judge's wig.

"Damn my eyes!" he said, with disgust all over his long, cruel face. "This place is full of stinking Franceys!"

The large fat Duchess in the portrait opposite was furious. She shook a pink first with diamond rings embedded in it. "And you took bribes, George Toller!" she screamed. "No Judge was ever greedier than you, nor hanged more poor souls who could not pay!"

At this, the people in the other portraits joined in by leaning out of their frames and yelling insults. "Drunk before breakfast!" somebody beside Heather screamed, and the person beside Robert howled, "And you are mutton dressed as lamb, madam!" Robert listened with his head on one side, trying to discover what made them hate one another so, but there was far too much noise.

Meanwhile, the fat Duchess was so angry that she hoisted one bulging leg over the edge of her frame, ready to climb down and go for Judge George Toller. As she did so, Mum came in at the other end of the Feud Room, leading a crowd of tourists.

"Here is what is called the Feud Room," Mum began. She stopped, gaping, as the Duchess hoisted her other leg across the frame and dropped to the floor with a wallop that rattled every piece of glass in the room.

"Now, eat your words, George Toller!" the Duchess screamed.

Behind Mum, everyone in the guided tour crowded through and stared at the Duchess. They seemed to think this was meant to be happening.

At this, Robert got the giggles. "What are they?" he asked. "How they gape! They are nothing but sheep!" He spread his hand out, laughing so much he had to hold his wrist with his other hand to keep it steady.

"No, don't!" Heather said, too late again.

The Feud Room was suddenly full of sheep. It was also suddenly full of Franceys and Tollers from past times, all jumping down from their frames to go on with their feud. The sheep ran and bleated and got in the way of people in red robes and black coats and blue brocade and embroidered waistcoats and huge rustling skirts with corsets that creaked. Each of these people had snatched up things from their portraits to use as weapons. Some were lucky enough to have been painted with sticks, or whips and parasols, and one man even had a sword, but that was knocked out of his hand by a small thin man who was belabouring everyone in sight with a huge book. The rest of them

60

hit one another with fans and embroidery frames and rolls of parchment and silken purses. Hats flew off, and wigs were knocked sideways.

In the midst of it all, Mum was standing holding a shepherd's crook, staring from the red, angry faces of the Tollers and the Franceys to the running, bleating sheep, and looking more bewildered than Heather had ever seen her.

"Oh, poor Mum!" Heather said. "Robert, stop it this instant!"

But Robert just ran away down the Long Gallery, laughing. Heather ran after him. He was not running very fast, because he kept doubling over to laugh, but he was very good at dodging. Heather almost caught him every time he stopped to laugh, but either he dodged, or the world tipped slightly as she put her hand out to grab him, and she knew that he had got away by magic. In spite of her annoyance, Heather almost laughed once or twice, because Robert so clearly thought of it as a game. She felt more as if she was chasing a small boy, instead of a young man who should have been old enough to know better.

Robert let Heather corner him, down the end of the Long Gallery at last. By this time the sheep had got out into the Long Gallery, too, and were running about on tottery little hooves crying, *"Baaa!"* in almost human voices. The polished floor was getting

sprinkled with their droppings, so that the fighting Tollers and Franceys, who had also spilled out of the Feud Room in a mass of bright-coloured clothes, kept slipping as they tried to hit one another. Heather saw the fat Duchess skid and fall flat on her back under the picture of Sir Francis Toller and

Queen Elizabeth I. She stayed there, puffing and mopping at her bleeding nose with a lace handkerchief. Mum was standing beside the Duchess, still holding the Shepherd's crook, looking round quite wildly.

Heather took hold of Robert's black silk shoulders and shook him. Doing that crumpled his crisp white collar, but Heather did not care. She felt like Robert's elder sister.

"Stop them! Turn them back!" she said. "Quickly, before Mum decides she's gone mad!"

"But you think of them as sheep yourself," Robert said. "I know you do."

Heather had to admit he was right. "Yes, but I know they're people really," she said. "They probably think they're mad, too. Turn them back."

"Now?" Robert asked pleadingly. He made his most charming smile at her. "But all will be back by sunset. Can they not wait?"

"No. Sunset's far too late at this time of year," Heather said. "Do it now. Do it or – or I shall never speak to you again!"

She said this because it was what she often said to Janine – not meaning it, of course – and it was the only threat she could think of. She was surprised how well it worked. Robert's eyes went big and sad. "Never?" he said.

"Never!" Heather shouted firmly, above the bleating and the yelling from the rest of the Long Gallery.

"Then I am gone maybe another hundred years," Robert said sadly. "Very well, I'll undo it, if you promise to speak to me again now, and again tomorrow."

"Of course I promise," Heather said.

Robert smiled, sighed and held his hand out. This time he tipped it the other way from usual, Heather noticed. Ordinariness swung back across her. The sheep stood up and were real people again, wandering round the Gallery with startled, rather prim looks, as if they had caught sight of something none of them wanted to know about. One or two people were irritably lifting their feet up and obviously wondering where they had trodden in a sheep dropping. Heather looked for the fat Duchess but she was not there at all. Nor were the other Tollers and Franceys. Nor were the wigs and hats that had been knocked off on to the floor.

"Are they all in their pictures again?" Heather asked.

"Yes, I swear it," Robert said.

"And what would happen if you held your hand out the other way up?" Heather asked. "Does that tip things too?"

Robert put that hand behind him. "Don't ask me to show you that," he said. "That is how my brother's wife came to hate me so."

Heather did not ask. She looked anxiously to see how Mum was instead. The only thing Robert seemed to have forgotten – apart from sheep droppings – was the shepherd's crook. Perhaps he wanted to show he still thought the tourists were sheep. Perhaps he meant it as a kindness. Anyway, Mum was still holding it, and leaning on it rather heavily, while the people from the guided tour slowly forgot they had been sheep and gathered round her, waiting for more of the talk.

"We are now in the Long Gallery," Mum said. She sounded a bit faint, but her voice seemed to come back as she explained how Sir Francis had built the Long Gallery because rooms like that were the height of fashion then.

"That is true, you know," Robert told Heather. "Shall we follow these sheep for a while? I would like to know the later history of my family and their house."

This suited Heather. That way she could keep an eye on both Mum and Robert. And she could be quite sure of not meeting Dad. The tours were arranged so that they went one after another, without ever meeting. Dad would be taking a tour either ahead of Mum's or behind. Heather was not ready to meet him yet. Dad asked such piercing questions and he was so full of common sense. She knew she had to make him *believe* when he did meet Robert, and there were a lot of things she wanted to think about first.

Heather thought and thought while they trailed behind the people who had been sheep and listened to Mum telling them things about the house. While she thought, she kept an eye on Robert, ready to grab his wrist if he showed any sign of spreading his hand out again, and she watched Mum quite as anxiously. She was glad to see that by the time they got to the Grand Saloon, Mum was explaining about the new fashion for Chinese decorations as if she had quite forgotten there had been sheep mixed with a fight in the Long Gallery. She was glad that Robert did not try to spread his hand out again. But she had not the foggiest idea what to do about him after this.

"This is boring," Robert whispered as everyone trooped after Mum into Lady Mary's music room. "Let us go to the watch-tower and find your father."

"OK," Heather said, rather relieved. The tower was probably a safe place, because she was fairly sure Dad would not be there. Anyway, she thought, it would have to do.

They slipped away from the back of the tour. Heather took Robert the long way round to the tower, to be quite sure of not meeting any other people. "I think," she said carefully, as they went, "it would be best if you let me speak to Dad first, before you talk to him. I know how to get him in the right mood. Suppose you were to keep out of sight. You could hide at the top of the tower."

"A good place," Robert agreed. "Is your father a witch-hater then?"

"More like someone who doesn't believe in them," Heather said.

Robert smiled, in a way that made Heather even less anxious for him to meet Dad. "I have met those, too, in my time," he said.

"I'll bring you some food and some blankets," Heather said. That was the only thing to do, she thought. Keep Robert hidden and hope she could work something out.

"Now food would be very welcome," Robert said.

They came clattering down the back stairs into the round room that had once been part of the castle. Heather hurried Robert to the tower stair. She had her hand on the red rope across it to unhook it, when Dad came hurrying through the round room the opposite way.

"Oh! Hi, Dad," Heather said awkwardly.

"Hi, sunshine," Dad said. "Don't take your friend up the tower now. It's nearly closing time."

"*Is* it?" Heather said. She was very surprised. The day had simply raced by.

"Yes, I'm sorry to disappoint your friend," Dad said, "but I wouldn't like to lock you both in when I lock this part. I'll be coming round with the keys in about ten minutes now."

While Dad was speaking, Heather had a sideways glimpse of Robert's hand spread out, and a tipping feeling. After that, however much she pushed her eyes sideways, all she could see was an empty stretch of whitewashed wall. "What friend?" she said, but inside she was saying frantically *Where is he? What has he done NOW?*

Dad looked at the empty part of the wall and blinked. "How odd!" he said. "I could have sworn you had a friend with you. It even struck me he had a sort of Jacobean look. Anyway, I'll see you at supper, sunshine." And he rushed away.

As soon as he was out of sight, Heather unhooked the red rope and raced round and round up the tower steps. At the top, she sagged with relief. Robert was sitting in the place she liked to sit herself, with his hands clasped round his knees, staring out at the hills and the patches of wood all lit golden green as the sun began to go down.

"You spoke to your father?" he said.

"Well, I – er – not yet. He was in a hurry," Heather explained.

"I left you alone to speak with him," Robert said reproachfully. "Where is the food you promised?"

"Coming up soon," Heather said. "But only if you stay *here* while I fetch it. You're not to disappear like that again! You give me heart attacks!"

Chapter Six

Heather plunged back down the tower stairs, knowing she only had about ten minutes, and not trusting Robert to stay there longer than that anyway. She raced through the old kitchen and into the new small one and opened the fridge. Bother. Only spam there, apart from raw food for supper. Heather collected the spam and the last of the bread and hurtled off to the tourist shop to catch Mrs Mimms before she went home.

Mrs Mimms was clearing up, and she was very puzzled. "Something's up today," she said. "I don't know! First there's half the people went home in the middle of the afternoon, just when they usually want to come in here for their ice-creams and their tins of fizz. My takings are right down."

"Oh, dear," Heather said guiltily. "Is it very bad?"

"Only so-so," Mrs Mimms said quite cheerfully. "It was a good morning, and Mr Mimms says most of them bought tickets to see round the house, even though they didn't use them. It makes you wonder what got into everyone."

"Do you think something frightened everyone?" Heather suggested, picking up two packets of biscuits and a bag of peanuts.

"Could be," said Mrs Mimms. "Mr Mimms says he kept getting complaints there were nudist boys chasing girls in nighties all over the woods. Someone came and told me that, too, and I told her not in *Castlemaine*. But someone else told your dad and he went out to look. He said *he* couldn't see a thing."

"Er – probably just some teenagers messing about," Heather said, guiltily adding crisps and popcorn to her pile of food.

"Bound to be," said Mrs Mimms. "Or people imagined it, like that new guide who swore to your dad there were sheep droppings all over the Long Gallery floor. Sheep, I told him. There's been no sheep near here for fifty years now! Next thing, I said to him, you'll be telling me you saw Wild Robert risen from his mound, treasure and all!"

Heather found her face had gone very hot. Knowing it must be bright red, she picked up a plastic bag labelled VISIT CASTLEMAINE and bent over it while she pushed her pile of food inside it. "Do you know all about Wild Robert then?" she asked.

"No more than most people in the village do," Mrs Mimms said. "I've only lived here half my life, after all. If you want to know about that old story, you should ask your friend Janine. Her folks have been in this area for centuries. And why are you taking all that food, Heather, may I ask?"

"Our fridge is empty," Heather said. "I didn't get much lunch."

"And you're acting as odd as the rest!" Mrs Mimms said. "You wouldn't believe the strange phone call I had a while back from Mrs McManus. Little as I like that woman, I think me and Mr Mimms better pop in on our way home and see if she's all right.

Sounds off her rocker to me – and I don't think I can let you have more than just one tin of coke, Heather."

Heather took a packet of cupcakes as well as the coke and pelted to the tower, clutching the bag to her. She was very glad to find that Robert was still there, wistfully watching the sun march through a tower of cloud, down towards the hills. He smiled at Heather when she came panting to the top of the stairs, and nodded out towards the view.

"Don't tell me," he said. "None of this is Castlemaine land any longer. Right?"

"Only the house is now," Heather said. She had not any breath to say more.

Robert spread his hand out towards the green landscape. Heather found she had stopped even being able to pant. She thought she really might have a heart attack. "In my time," Robert said, "everything a man could see from the top of this tower was Castlemaine land." He took his hand back, sadly. "If I made it mine, it wouldn't last," he said. "Where is the food you promised?"

"Here," gasped Heather. She was breathless with relief now.

Robert smiled quite heartily. "My hunger is three hundred and fifty years old. I feel like an empty rain barrel," he said.

Heather had to leave as soon as she had given him the bag of food, for fear of getting locked up in the old castle when Dad did his rounds with the keys. She told herself that this would mean that Robert was safely locked up in the tower, where there was no one to turn into sheep or dogs, at least until tomorrow morning. The trouble was, she did not believe this. She was fairly sure Robert could easily burst the locked doors open if he wanted to. Or, if he did decide to stay in the tower, he could probably work any magic he wanted to from there. Heather just had to hope he would decide to stay there quietly until she had spoken to Dad. He seemed to trust her to do that. And this was another thing that made Heather uncomfortable, because she was still not sure what she was going to say to Dad.

At the moment, however, it was Mum she wanted to see. It took Heather a while to track Mum down. She found her, at last, in the small kitchen, starting to get supper ready. Heather at once began to help, without even being asked, so that she could go on keeping an eye on Mum.

Mum seemed all right, but she kept darting alarmed looks at the shepherd's crook, which was propped up in a corner. From time to time she said, in a puzzled way, "It's too early in the season to be overworked. I wonder if I'm going down with something."

Each time Heather said, quickly and firmly, "Of course not. There's nothing wrong with you at all."

"You *are* being kind," Mum said at last. "How grown-up and considerate you're getting, Heather."

Heather found her face getting hot again. It was Robert who was making her feel that way. When she thought about him, she almost felt like a mother herself – a mother with the kind of naughty small boy who pulls down piles of food in the supermarket and the mother has to pay for it. "The potatoes are nearly done," she said, to take her mind off it. "How long is supper going to be? I can hardly wait."

This was true. After just one sandwich for lunch, Heather was starving. Strawberries do not fill a person up.

"Not long now," Mum said. "I like suppertime, too. It's the only time of day when we can be a proper family. You can go and jangle the bell for Dad, while I dish the meat up."

When supper was on the table, Heather fell on it as if she was the one who had not eaten for three hundred and fifty years. But she knew she had to talk to Dad about Robert. So, as soon as she felt a little less empty, she started the talk by saying, "Dad, you know all the history of Castlemaine, don't you?"

"I've read up a fair bit," Dad admitted. "Why?"

"Have you read about anyone called Robert Toller?" Heather said. "About three hundred and fifty years ago."

As if this was a cue, the room tipped a bit and the spoons clattered on the table. Mum put her hand to her head. Heather jumped nervously. For a moment she wondered if Robert was actually in the room, invisible. But when she thought about it, she knew that the tipping had a sort of far-away feel to it. Robert was still in the tower. He was just reminding her he was there. She looked at Dad. Dad did not seem to notice anything unusual at all. He was frowning, trying to think of the Robert Toller Heather meant.

"He may have been the youngest son of the second Sir Francis," Heather said. It was a guess, but she thought it was right. Robert had talked as if his brothers were older than he was.

"Oh *him*!" said Dad. He smiled. "You're thinking of your treasure again, aren't you? You mean the young man who was executed for witchcraft?"

"*Executed*!" Heather exclaimed. Was Robert really dead, then, she wondered, without knowing he was?

There was another tipping. Saucepans joggled on the stove. In spite of her horror and alarm, Heather began to be annoyed. Robert really was like a naughty small boy in some ways. Why couldn't he leave her alone to talk to Dad? She was *trying*, wasn't she?

"Go on," she said to Dad.

"Well, it's a strange story," Dad said. "Robert's father, the younger Francis, met some kind of very odd woman and married her as his second wife. I suspect she was a gypsy. Nobody seems to have known where she came from and she ran away quite soon, leaving the boy with his father. And it looks as if Robert inherited some peculiar gifts from his mother. The records say that when he was small and fell down and hurt himself, all the church bells rang."

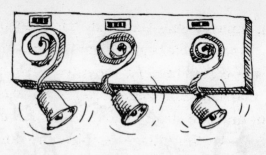

There was a faint chiming from the corner of the kitchen. Heather turned round, with the back of her neck prickling, to see the row of little bells there, which the Franceys used to ring when they wanted a servant, swaying back and forth. Robert was still at his tricks.

"I'm sure that was absolute nonsense," Dad said, "but in those days it was enough to start all the people in the village talking about witchcraft. Robert's father wouldn't listen to a word of it. He gave the boy anything he wanted and refused to believe there was any difference between Robert and his two elder brothers."

"So he always got away with it," Heather murmured.

The bells were still chiming. Mum was watching the salt cellar roll slowly down the length of the table, leaving a trail of salt. "I think," Mum said nervously, "that I may be going down with flu. Or something."

"No, you're not," said Heather. "There's nothing wrong with any bit of you. I know. So Robert must have grown up very spoilt and babyish. Go on, Dad."

Mum smiled feebly. Dad said, "He probably did, Heather. And trouble began after his father died and James, the eldest brother, inherited Castlemaine. James married Eliza Francey. Eliza was very religious and she clearly hated young Robert. She tried to make the village people burn him as a witch, but the village people said they were scared even to try, because of what Robert might do to them. And it does look as if Robert did something to Eliza. Next morning she woke screaming, saying that Robert had put her in hell all that night."

"With his hand the other way up," said Heather. "If he did, I bet she deserved it. And?"

"So Eliza made James bring in a bishop who was an uncle of hers," Dad said. "And the record says the bishop cleansed Castlemaine. It doesn't say how. It just says that Robert was buried in the grounds. They didn't let witches have a grave in the churchyard, you know."

"So it *doesn't* say the bishop had Robert executed!" Heather said.

"Not in so many words," Dad said. "But you don't bury people unless they're dead, Heather."

"But I think they *did*! Poor Robert!" said Heather. She finished her pudding in three mouthfuls. Janine would know. And the key to the tower was in the living room, hanging on the board above the telephone. "Can I use the phone?"

Chapter Seven

Dad was amused. "Phone?" he said. "Heather, this was hundreds of years ago! I don't think today's bishop knows anything about it. Besides, bishops are busy men."

"I don't want to phone a bishop," Heather said. "I want to ring Janine."

"Then don't talk for more than twenty minutes," said Mum. "It's getting near your bedtime. Look how dark it is."

Heather knew this was just one of Mum's unfair excuses. The kitchen faced away from the evening sun, so it was always dark around supper time. But Mum worried about phone bills, particularly after a difficult day. "I'll be ever so quick," Heather promised forgivingly. She bounced up from the table and hurtled into the living room, where, sure enough, the light was strong pink sunset. It coloured Heather's hand orange as she dialled Janine's number.

"Janine," she said, when Janine was called to the

phone, "tell me every bit you know about Wild Robert. It's important."

"I told you most of it," Janine said. "My mum and dad may know a bit more, I suppose. Want me to go and ask them?"

"Yes," said Heather.

Janine was gone quite a long time. Heather waited, and watched the sun colour the row of keys on the board above the phone a deeper and deeper pink. After a bit, she took down the key to the tower and held it ready. She would have to go and fetch Robert to the kitchen when Janine had told her the rest of the story. That would stop him playing any more tricks, and it would show Mum and Dad he was real. She just had to hope that what Janine told her would help her to explain about him.

"Well," said Janine's voice at last. She sounded out of breath. "Sorry to be so long. Mum told me to go next door and ask my gran and Gran does talk a lot. Anyway, this is the story. Don't blame me. It's what my gran said. She says Wild Robert's father had a wife, but he loved another woman who was – well sort of – well Gran called her a fairy." Janine sounded really embarrassed having to say this. "And this other woman was Wild Robert's mother. Wild Robert's father married her after his wife died, when Wild Robert was a baby. But Gran says the rest of the family was furious, and hated the new wife so much,

and were so nasty to her that she ran away and left Wild Robert to grow up by himself at Castlemaine. And it wasn't long before he was working all sorts of magic. And when he grew older, he read books and studied and found out how to do even more magic.

Gran says his father was ever so proud of him, but the only thing was—" Janine got embarrassed again and stopped.

"Go *on*!" said Heather.

"She," said Janine, "his mother, you know, was only half

of Wild Robert, so he couldn't work magic all the time, only during the daytime. And the rest of the family knew this. So when his father died and his brothers wanted to get rid of Wild Robert, Gran says they waited until it was dark. Then they cut his heart out and put it into a silver box where he couldn't get at it and buried both parts of him in that mound."

"How – *awful!*" said Heather. No wonder Wild Robert had that way of looking hurt and trying to hide it. He must have liked and trusted his brothers.

"People *were* awful in those days," Janine said.

"So is that all?" said Heather.

"No," said Janine. "There's a bit more." She was embarrassed again. "They say that because of his mother being – being what she was, Wild Robert couldn't really die. They say that if someone calls his name by the mound, specially if it's around mid-day, Wild Robert will answer and come out. Gran told me quite a few stories of how people called him and then ran like mad when he appeared."

"Oh, dear!" said Heather.

So Robert had been out before. It was odd the way he didn't seem to remember. But he was, Heather thought, most of the time half dead, the way he was half alive. And every time he came out, it must have been all new to him – a new time in history and a new, fresh memory of how the people he had loved had tried to kill him. Heather thought that in Robert's place, she wouldn't have behaved even half as well. She would have done more than play tricks. She would have tried to break the place up. And she thought that, in spite of being a spoiled baby, this must mean that Robert was a nice person underneath.

Janine must have thought that Heather was getting upset by the story. "Yes, but it's all right," she said soothingly. "It's not really a ghost story, because his power ends at sunset. Gran says he has to go back to his mound and his heart as soon as the sun goes down."

"*Does* he?" Heather shot a frantic look at the dark pink light slanting through the window.

"Definitely," said Janine. "That's the treasure they talk about – the silver box with his heart in it."

"Sorry, Janine," Heather said. "I have to go now. I need to go up the tower at once. See you as soon as my bike's mended."

She hurled the phone down and raced back to the kitchen. She could tell Robert was up to more tricks in there, because there were now strangled-sounding yelps and whines coming from someone. Heather was afraid Robert had made Mum really ill.

But the sounds were coming from the large mottled dog. Mrs McManus was standing, planted like a massive tree, just inside the back door,

blocking Heather's way to the tower. She was
holding a rope that was tied round the dog's neck
and the dog kept straining to get free.

"And he comes from nowhere in the middle of
the afternoon," Mrs McManus was telling Mum and
Dad.

Heather looked at the dog's mottled face. The
dog looked back accusingly.

"And *round* the hoose and *round* the hoose and pawing at the door to come in," said Mrs McManus. "And not a soul in the village owns to him any more than you do! I'm thinking someone of those tourists kidnapped Mr McManus and left me this beast in his place."

"Well, I admit I haven't seen your husband since this morning," Dad said, "but that strikes me as an odd thing for a kidnapper to do – where are you going, Heather?"

"Just for something I left – on the tower steps," Heather said, waving the key as she tried to squeeze past Mrs McManus on the other side from the dog.

"No, Heather," Mum said. "Bedtime." She took firm hold of Heather's arm.

"Oh, *please*!" Heather said, wriggling.

"Do as your mother says," said Dad.

As he spoke, the sun must have set. Mrs McManus cried out. She was suddenly holding Mr McManus by a rope round his neck. Mr McManus stood up and wrenched at the rope, staring at Heather in the same cringing, glaring way in which he had stared at her when he was a dog. Heather knew she had made an enemy for life. But she had known that before. She almost could not think of Mr McManus for the sadness that came over her.

"I must say that I don't understand this," Dad said.

Understatement of the year! Heather thought.

"Oh!" cried Mrs McManus. "I have come over queer! How could I lead my own man on a rope like a dog!" She sank into the nearest kitchen chair. Mr McManus flopped on to another, rubbing angrily at his neck. Mum forgot she was sending Heather to bed and hurried to put the kettle on for tea.

Nobody seemed to know what to say. They waited awkwardly while the kettle began to sing. And while they waited, Heather thought she heard noises outside the back door. It sounded mostly like scared whispering. Just as she thought she ought to say something about the sounds, somebody knocked timidly on the door.

Dad opened it. Outside was a group of white-faced, tired teenagers. All their hairstyles were in a mess. Some of them had torn clothes. This made them look a great deal younger, somehow, and not at all alarming.

"Sorry to trouble you," one of the girls said politely.

"We saw the light," said a boy.

"And – er – we don't know what happened but the coach we came in went and left without us," said another girl.

"We – er – we sort of lost track of time," another boy explained.

"You'd better come in and have some tea," Dad said. "Heather, get out eight more cups. We'll see if we can sort something out. Any of you have parents we can phone?"

The teenagers crowded timidly in and stood leaning against the furniture. Mr and Mrs McManus glared at them, but they said nothing. Heather laid the key to the tower down on the table and went round with cups of tea, feeling sadder and sadder. Janine's Gran was right. Wild Robert's power really did end at sunset. He must be back in his mound now. Heather had to admit that this did solve everyone's problems, but she still wished it had not happened. It seemed so unfair on Robert.

Then, when the teenagers crowded into the living room with Dad to phone their families and Mum at

last sent Heather to bed, Heather remembered that Wild Robert had made her promise to speak to him again tomorrow. He had known. He knew he would have to go back to the mound at sunset, and he had planned for it. This made Heather feel much better. She climbed up the stairs to her little room in a corner of the old castle, smiling. Robert was full of tricks. Tomorrow she would understand him better. She would manage to explain him to Mum and Dad. She could start teaching him to be a modern person.

Heather fell asleep thinking of ways she might even rescue the treasure that was really Wild Robert's heart...

Order Form

To order direct from the publishers, just make a list of the titles you want and fill in the form below:

Name ....

Address ....

....

....

Send to: Dept 6, HarperCollins Publishers Ltd, Westerhill Road, Bishopbriggs, Glasgow G64 2QT.

Please enclose a cheque or postal order to the value of the cover price, plus:

UK & BFPO: Add £1.00 for the first book, and 25p per copy for each additional book ordered.

Overseas and Eire: Add £2.95 service charge. Books will be sent by surface mail but quotes for airmail despatch will be given on request.

A 24-hour telephone ordering service is available to holders of Visa, MasterCard, Amex or Switch cards on 0141- 772 2281.

Collins
An *Imprint of* HarperCollins*Publishers*